The Journey of Captain Michael Stanvic

The Journey of Captain Michael Stanvic

A PIRATE'S QUEST

Christopher Swank &

Michelle Vickery

To order additional copies of this book, contact:
Xlibris Corporation
1-888-795-4274
www.Xlibris.com
Orders@Xlibris.com
54196

Contents

This book is dedicated to our little pirates who not only use imagination at play but force us to use ours also. We love you forever.

Sherri Lynne
Christine Lynne
Kasey Lee
Stanley Michael

Introduction

Captain Michael Stanvic was born in the small town of Christinville. His father was a logger and had been almost all his life. Captain Stanvic used to, as a small child, go to work with his dad and help him out. He used to pretend that long sticks were a cutlass and that he was defending his grandfather's ship. However, as he had gotten older he decided logging would not be the life for him.

Captain Stanvic's grandfather had been a rather wealthy man. That was mainly due to him being a pirate. Before gambling his riches all away on games of poker, he had a large sea chest full of gold bars and jewelry. Piracy was about the only way, at that time, for a man to become wealthy.

Chapter 1

Finding the Map

Captain Stanvic's grandfather had made a promise to him that when he passed on that he would leave him a great wealth. Captain Stanvic did not know that it would end up being in the form of a treasure map at the bottom of his grandfather's secret chest.

Therefore, upon finding this map, Captain Stanvic would begin preparing for his long journey to finding this hidden treasure. Poor Captain Stanvic did not realize it would take so much effort to find a buried treasure. Nor did he realize what dangers could be lurking ahead of his voyage.

He began by placing his clothing into a large cedar chest. Next, he went into the pantry and began filling wooden boxes with non-perishable items such as beans, rice, salt etc . . . He knew he would have to be well prepared for this journey because once it began there would be no turning back.

He scratched his head and looked steadily around wondering if he had forgotten anything. He thought to his self "this is going to be a wonderful adventure."

Before leaving for the port to load his vessel, he visited his mother and father promising them that he would return home safely and bring to them great wealth. He kissed them both and left for the port

As planned earlier, Captain Stanvic's shipmates were waiting for him at the fish market near the Port of St. Kasen. They all eagerly greeted him as they began to load their belongings onto *the Blue Pearl.* They were all excited about the journey, in which they were embarking upon,

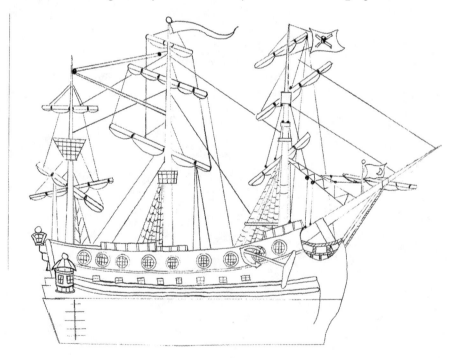

Chapter 2

The Ship Leaves Port

After loading the ship, each of the shipmates was given a task they were to perform on this journey. Sherlin was given the chore of being "master of the galley." Everyone knew that this was the job for her, because of her marvelous ability to spice and season foods fit for the Queen. Some of them jokingly say that Sherlin could even make a rat tasty.

Sherlin was from St. Kasen Island. Her mother had taught her how to cook good food in high hopes that one day she would cook for the Queen. That was not what Sherlin wanted—all she wanted was to become a pirate, and she intended on showing everyone that she had just what it takes to be one.

Fredrick was to be in charge of raising and lowering the sails. He was given this job because of his mighty strength. The deckhands knew very little about Fredrick, except that he lived inland and that he had a wife and two children. He was an exceptional hand but rarely spoke.

Delphin was to raise and lower the flags on the ship. He was also to keep the deck of the ship clean and clutter free. Delphin had been born deaf, but you still had to think that he knew what was going on at all times if you had ever sat and watched his facial expressions.

Delphin had just recently come to work for Captain Stanvic after his father had been killed in a mining accident. His mother was now alone to care for her seven other children. Delphin was depending on this treasure hunt as much as any of the other shipmates were.

"All other shipmates are to perform the same duties they have always performed," announced Captain Stanvic, "let's get this mighty ship sailing!"

As the ship begins to leave, everyone was hanging over the balconies and waving their goodbyes to their families and friends back at the port. The ship was filled with absolute excitement.

Merchant ships were sailing in from the west bringing into the port fresh food, spices, and other provisions such as textiles, cotton, and wool. Anglers were bringing in "the catch of the day" and collecting their pay for a hard days work. The dolphins were playing so gracefully around the dock and piers. The seagulls were flying stylishly overhead.

The sun was at high noon that day as they headed into the Raven Ocean. The wind was blowing steadily as Fredrick began to raise the sails. Delphin was preparing the flags to fly from the huge masts on *the Blue Pearl*. These flags were enormous in size. Two of which were friendly country flags and one of which was a pirate flag. None more suiting than it was for this ship.

The ship's mates were all standing outside in attention to the far horizon. Some were looking through portholes assuring Captain Stanvic that there were no dangers in sight ahead. Captain Stanvic was feeling more at ease on this trip after recalling earlier his previous voyage, which had been one of many dangers.

Chapter 3

Suppertime in the Galley

The dolphins from near the port had been following the ship and jumping gracefully in and out of the water. They were also flapping their flippers as if they were waving to the shipmates abroad. The mammals playful chirping was a pleasant sound to everyone. They were definitely the most beautiful creatures in the oceans. They were carefree and magnificent!

The island they had left behind was nothing more than a mere speck of land now. They were beginning to see Blackcut Mountains in the near distance. Blackcut Mountains were beautiful in the summertime. It was nice to see the snow capped mountains on a hot blistery day and imagining yourself sitting at the top of them.

However, Blackcut Mountains was lurking with danger. The Kasadonians in a battle with the Cindivians had captured Blackcut Mountains in 1598. The Kasadonians were originally from Melistiqville. The Kasadonians had been banned from their country after losing a battle with the Dionians.

The Kasadonians were mainly sheep owners. The Kasadonians were blessed with large herds of black sheep. They would use the sheep for their beautiful wool and for keeping the pastures neatly grazed. According to the townsfolk back at St. Kasen, the unscrupulous Kasadonians would tie lanterns to the necks of their sheep and walk them along the high dunes to mock the lights of boats at anchor. This would cause ships to run aground, where they would then steal their cargo.

Sherlin had come up on deck to announce that it was now suppertime. She had prepared a tasty meal of fish and rice. The fish had been lightly salted, peppered, and cooked on top a boucan located at the stern of the ship. She was always great at cooking any kind of fish. The buccaneers originally engineered boucans and were used for smoking dried meat.

As the men sit down to eat, John began telling his tall tales of his early years of piracy. Everyone listened closely, imagining their selves playing the roles of undefeated treasure hunters, overcoming extreme obstacles and celebrating great victory at the end of each voyage.

Spirits were being generously passed around the tables as the men were dancing unsteadily around the ships bottom deck. Card games were being played for pieces of eight a hand. Men were bellowing shanties of little meaning watching their shipmates lose their money unwittingly to Pegleg Dean. Back in the days Pegleg Dean (at a price of course) would teach young apprentices the basics of winning a hand or two.

Feathers, Captain Stanvic's parrot, sat back in his cage atop a table located in the center of the galley. He was Captain Stanvic's pride and joy. Captain Stanvic had purchased Feathers from a man who lived in craigenstan. Captain Stanvic had fallen in love with Feathers as soon as he laid his eyes upon him. He had offered the man 10 pieces of gold in which the man readily accepted the offer.

Captain Stanvic was unaware that Feathers could be taught to speak. He had laid down one night and had told Feathers good night as always and much to his surprise; Feathers replied, "Good night, Good night." Since then Captain Stanvic along with other shipmates have been teaching Feathers a vast list of words to speak.

Chapter 4

The Battle of Blackcut Mountain

As nightfall began to set, the pirates were changing guards on the ships upper deck. Blackcut Mountain was becoming decreasingly visible with a heavy fog that had begun to set in. The fog on this night was mysteriously grim. To some of the shipmates it posed a grave danger of lost visibility.

They were within three nautical miles from Blackcut Mountain and worry began to sit in that the Kasadonians might be using the fog to their advantage. Not only had the Kasadonians relocated to Blackcut Mountains, they were slowly killing the few remaining Elsians, who had occupied the Blackcut Mountains since the 1450's.

Captain Stanvic had turned the captain duties over to Leevin for the night upon retiring to his humble abode located underneath the ship's upper deck. Before retiring for the night, he lit his reading lamp and pulled out his favorite novel written by Gottfried Alberti called *Hidden Dangers of the Sea*. This novel had put him to bed many a cold night.

Leevin had never been in charge of such a mighty ship and was leery of what might be lurking ahead. Within one and a half nautical miles, Leevin began see what appeared to be boats at anchor. How excited he was to be so close to landfall again.

Sherlin had come up to the Captain's quarters to tell Leevin goodnight and to see that all was well, when straight ahead she noticed the strange lights that were waiting up on shore. She screamed in horror at Leevin to stop the ship while she ran across deck to tell the men to drop anchor before getting any closer than they were already to the strange lights.

Sure enough, the Kasadonians were waiting in the shadows with cannons loaded eagerly awaiting the ship to come ashore. The men on the top deck began taking aim towards the shore to prepare for a battle they hoped they were not about to be in.

Sherlin had gone to awaken Captain Stanvic. He ran to the deck and stood in attention with the other men to see if the Kasadonians were about to fire upon them. Sure enough, loud blasts began and the water around their ship was splashing with cannon balls everywhere. No one had warned them that the Kasadonians were such a poor shot. This would go to explain why they had been defeated and exiled from Melistiqville.

Upon their need to fire upon our ship, we felt that we should return a few of the cannonballs to them. Ross, who was our best artillery expert, fired a two ball chained cannon right into the midst of the Kasadonians that had fired at us. The Kasadonians did not take long to retreat back into their properties.

Captain Stanvic was pleased in the way that his crew had handled that situation. He invited them all to the galley where they were to be served biscuits and spiced rum. He and Feathers then retired back to his sleeping quarters.

"Good night Feathers" said Captain Stanvic.

"Good night, good night" Feathers squawked.

Chapter 5

The Shipmates Retire for the Night

Most everyone on board the ship retired to their hammocks for a couple of hours of sleep. (Captains always slept in sleeping quarters and the hired help would sleep in hammocks.) Bristol and Ross returned up deck to continue their nightly duties.

Bristol had been born an only child to a young Catholic couple. His grandfather on his father's side, like Captain Stanvic's, had also been a pirate. His father and mother had been attacked and brutally killed by a group of old sea dogs. His grandfather had cheated out of a few hundred gold pieces in a game of cards.

His grandfather fled to Palm Island in order to evade his ex-pirate mates and to try to make things right by raising his grandson in a safer environment. However, his grandfather turned to his old ways and he ended up raising Bristol as a young pirate.

The seas around them remained calm the night was beginning to grow shorter. Bristol and Ross began trading stories of the dangers they had encountered in their earlier days on the high seas.

"I once met a mad man while sailing near the Breakaway Islands" said Ross.

"Really?" asked Bristol.

"Yes, indeed I did," answered Ross. "He had a peg leg on his right, an eye patch on his right eye, and one hook on the left and many a scar across his face."

That's a great deal of injuries to a man of fortune," Bristol said.

"He had received these injuries from Captain Smith for whom he had worked all his life for," said Ross. "Captain Smith had whacked off his arm and leg with his cutlass and had caused blindness in the one eye and the scaring up his face with his cat of nine tails" he had gone on to add.

"That Captain Smith sounds as though he was a forcefully cruel pirate," said Bristol.

"Yes he was, and if you ask me I think he should have been keelhauled and thrown into Davy Jones' locker," Ross answered. "At one time there was a great bounty hanging on his head."

"Makes us feel fortunate to have Captain Stanvic over this ship," Bristol said. "That is right" Ross exclaimed! "That's right," he repeated.

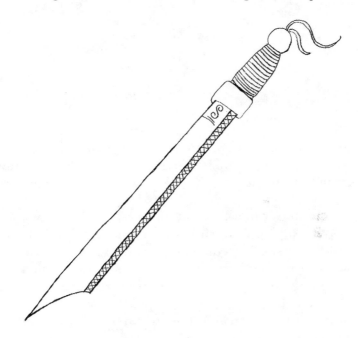

Chapter 6

A Mutineer on Board

The sun was beginning to rise in the east. The men from down below the deck were returning to their jobs. Some with hangovers and some were just grouchy from either lack of sleep and some were just naturally grouchy.

Delphin, the ships cabin boy and flagman, had began swabbing the decks to keep the boards from shrinking and letting in water. Off to his right he could see a small document that someone must have dropped. Delphin picked it up and knew that it must be of some importance to someone. He returned his cleaning cloths back to the bucket of water he had been using and began looking for Captain Stanvic.

Captain Stanvic opened it and snorted in horror. He was not sure who had brought this onto the ship, but he was certain to find out when he opened the letter. Captain Stanvic proceeded to the larboard side of the ship in which he demanded that all crewmates join him immediately.

"Ahoy there, me hearties, today it saddens me to know that there is a traitor amidst our ship" explains Captain Stanvic. "Among us is a privateer who has been sent by Sir Lance Pace," he says, "sent to overtake our ship and deliver us all to be branded and hanged."

The pirates broke out into a loud roar. They were all looking at each other and in their minds convincing themselves that the man standing next to them was the guilty rat. Captain Stanvic pulled from his coat pocket a worn piece of paper and holding it up for everyone to see.

"This, he says is the sworn approval of attack released by Sir Lance Pace." "On the inside of this despicable document it is addressed to Privateer Wm. E. Shuvell" explains Captain Stanvic.

Privateer Wm. Shuvell, Defender of Peace,
Your application made unto me for Licence
to arm, furnish, and equip the Ship Blaze of Glory,
You and your ships mates have been granted rights
by His Majesty, to attack and seize all Captains and
Crewmenbers of the Blue Pearl in which His Majesty
will reward to you 2 lbs. gold dust for delivering them
alive, 1 lb. if they are delivered dead, and 1/4 lb. if they
are delivered damaged.
Given under my hand this the 16th day of July, 1615.
By His Majesty's Command
Sir Lance Pace

My thoughts are with you.

"This document has caused great scrutiny to my ships mates," he says. "Privateer Shuvell is to be taken to the brig from which he will be guarded day in and day out" he adds, "and at exactly dusk we shall all gather in the galley to vote in determining Privateer Shuvell's fate."

Privateer Wm. E. Shuvell had come from King Island and had come onto the ship after replying to a flyer that he had found at a local merchant stand in Stanson. He had figured that would be the easiest way to overcome the ship and collect his bounty.

The bounty of which had been placed on Captain Stanvic and his ships mates' heads was in an amount of 2 pounds of gold dust if delivered to Sir Lance Pace with all of them alive. 1 pound of gold dust if any was killed. ¼ lb. gold dust if damaged prior to delivery.

Chapter 7

The Fate of Privateer Wm. E. Shuvell

Parrot Landing was ahead to the east approximately 10 nautical miles. This was the home of the free pirates. These pirates had saved themselves from hanging by promising to join Christianity and never return to piracy so long as they lived. They were branded with a large letter "P" on their backs so that if they did backslide they would definitely face being scorned and hanged.

The sun was beginning to fade and everyone was headed to the galley to eat some of Sherlin's fish stew and to vote on the fate of Privateer Wm. E. Shuvell's fate. The mood in the galley tonight was one of anger and frustration. They felt the King had chosen them to die.

"Ahoy!" says Captain Stanvic leading the ships mates into a discussion of Privateer Wm. E. Shuvell's fate. "Tonight, as we all know, we have a very important decision to gather," he says. "Privateer Shuvell befriended us!" Captain Stanvic yells loudly. "He has been ordered to have us destroyed by hanging," he adds, "so do we return the favor and make him walk the plank or do we maroon him to a desolated island in which he could use his privateer expertise to escape?" Captain Stanvic asks. "There will not be any discussion on the matter, so if everyone is ready let's now take a vote."

"All of you, who are in favor of Privateer Wm. E. Shuvell walking the plank at exactly midnight, please make yourself known by raising your hand and saying aye, aye!" Captain Stanvic proclaimed.

"All of you now who are opposed to Privateer Wm. E. Shuvell walking the plank and being marooned please make yourself known by raising your hand and saying nay." Captain Stanvic continues.

"Very well, and justly deserving I might add, Privateer Wm. E. Shuvell is hereby sentenced by the ships mates on board *the Blue Pearl* to death by walking the plank at exactly midnight tonight" bellows Captain Stanvic, "our pity now lies upon him and may God have mercy on his soul."

The men finished their supper and unlike the night before in which they had danced and drank merrily, they returned to the deck and continued with their work. The silence upon the ship was eerie and the men were now feeling uneasy about their journey to this hidden treasure.

The men were beginning to think in ways they should not. That if Privateer Wm. E. Shuvell had been ordered by Sir. Lance Pace to overtake this ship, then the question now arising amongst them was who else among them could also be involved.

Chapter 8

Riding the Storm Out

The sound of Thunderbolt Rising was becoming increasingly louder. The seas waters were beginning to become choppy. The ship was beginning to rock from side to side. Light sprinkles of rainfall could be felt from time to time. The sky was lighting up as if a huge lantern had been put up there to brighten our surroundings. It was beautiful but yet most dangerous.

Leevin was now in charge for steering the ship. He began to navigate the ship leeward. Fredrick had been fighting the sail for quiet some time now. Delphin began to take in the flags in fear of them blowing off their post.

Captain Stanvic awakened from all the commotion above deck. He quickly gathered his over clothes and hurriedly ran to the deck.

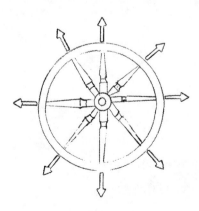

"Everyone, turn to!" yelled Captain Stanvic. "Fredrick, take in!" he screamed.

"Avast Leevin, we must let down sea anchors to slow the ship" he ordered. "Slow the rudders or will surely break the keel."

The rough waters were beating incessantly against the starboard and the larboard sides. The men were working relentlessly, steadily bailing water from the ships quarters. At the fore of the ship Leevin and Captain Stanvic worked together to keep the boat steady.

The harsh storm had vanished nearly as quickly as it had appeared. The ships mates were all joining in on swabbing the top deck so that no more water would seep into the quarters of the ship. They made plans to caulk all the boards when the morning sun came up.

Chapter 9

Pace Walks the Plank

At nearly midnight, Captain Stanvic ordered Privateer Shuvell fetched and brought to the stern of the ship. This was where he would be made to walk the plank. Up until this day, no one had ever been ordered to walk the plank on *the Blue Pearl*.

John was chosen to place a blindfold around Privateer Shuvell's eyes. His arms were tied behind him and a cinder block attached to each ankle. He then led him to a flight of ten steps. At the top of the steps rested an iron pressed platform. It was here that he would be asked to begin walking. He did with sheer poise and never once showed any sign of distress. When he hit the water, he was gone. He is now located in bottom of Davy Jones' locker.

The shipmates except for the two night watchers and Leevin returned to their hammocks to retire for the rest of the night. The wind was still blowing a bit. The shipmates were resolute in staying put for the night. They had ended up very near Moon Bay when the storm had ended.

Everyone was looking forward to making it to the Merchant Reload. Their provisions had been depleted rapidly. About all that was left in the pantry were beans, rice, and very little dried meats.

Getting the marketers to sell to them would probably be some sort of a problem. It normally was. They always ended up robbing them and taking what they needed. They did not at all take kindly to the pirates coming anywhere near them. They knew they would lose all their goods to the pirates stealing it all from them. They were almost to the point that Leepers Plantation, located north of them, were threatening to cut their supplies off if they did not find a way to stop them. They did not realize the solution to the problem was actually quiet simple to resolve. They had to quit trying to sell the goods to them without marking the prices so extremely high.

The shipmates had a plan to enforce before making it to Leepers Plantation. They would simply drop anchor when they made it to Leepers Plantation. Their plan included making a mad dash to collect whatever provisions they could in a short amount of time. A couple of guardsmen would stay on board preparing to cover them with fire if attacked.

Chapter 10

The Raid on Leepers Plantation

The sounds of loud snoring were enough to make anyone laugh. The men had worked hard today and they were very tired. Getting to sleep at night was almost a blessing to them.

At the sound of the crow, everyone began to show leg. Today would be a very important day. They would navigate to within one and a half nautical miles of Leepers Plantation. This mission was very important to this expedition. It would make or break the rest of this ship's journey.

The Jolly Roger was taken down and a friendly flag featuring the Stanson emblem temporarily replaced it. Anchors were being prepared to let down. Tackle was being brought out of the stores in case any of the shipmates had to be rescued from the waters. The men who were to stay on board headed to the Magazine to supply themselves with gunpowder and armaments. Surely, everyone would be able to take on this mission as planned.

Small rowing boats were being let down into the now shallow waters. Several heavy anchors were dropped from the stern to hold the boat steady. One at a time pirates began to leap into the water and swim hastily to the small rowing boats.

Quickly and strongly the pirates rowed up to shore. Slinging their paddles to the bottoms of the boats, they were jumping from the rowboats and tying their boats to the nearby trees.

The pirates were running in different directions with each of them knowing which plot of the plantation was their responsibility to steal loot.

The fruit trees were important especially the citrus fruit trees which were thought to prevent scurvy. It was actually a great time to be looking for these fruit trees because this was the season in which oranges, limes, lemons, and bananas were harvested.

A great deal of the men was interested in filling their loot bags with grapes. That was because the grapes in Leepers Plantation were known to make the best wine. As we all know, the pirates all loved the spirits regardless of what it was or what its ingredients were.

Fredrick raided the pigpens because he was the strongest of them all. He could wrestle a sow and have it hogtied in five seconds. This time he had six pigs tied and hung from a log that he would rest across the back of his neck and shoulders. He made it back to shore in less than 5 minutes and had the pigs loaded into his rowing boat. He then made his way back on board *the Blue Pearl*.

Delphin climbed into an orange tree on the outside of the orange grove. He did not want to stand on a ladder because of his inability to hear. Climbing up in the tree would help him to see what he could not hear down below him. He filled his loot bag and began to descend the tree. Out of the corner of his eyes, he noticed a small boy running and waving his arms at some men across the groves. Delphin knew what that meant and he made haste getting back to his rowing boat and getting back to the ship.

After being hoisted back on board, he was waving his arms uncontrollably at Captain Stanvic and pointing to the groves. It did not take long for them to figure that one out. Every rowboat that had been sent out to shore was now heading back to the ship.

Gunfire began to fly out in all directions. The artillerymen on the ship were firing over their own shipmates heads protecting them from the rapid gunfire coming from Leepers Plantation. The ship began firing cannonballs onto the shoreline backing the plantation men away from their fellow pirates.

As the men were pulled up, Sherlin began to yell for help. Christen had been shot in his left lower leg. Christen was shaking his head with disbelief that he had received another wound on another journey. After losing his right arm in a sword fight several years ago, Christen had since wised up on his defense strategies; it proved to be useless this day.

Christen had sailed many a journey with Captain Stanvic and it was he who had ask Christen to come on this journey. Captain Stanvic had felt bad about Christen losing his arm years earlier. He had thought it was only fitting to ask him along on this journey for such a great fortune to share in.

Dr. Agnes was the medic on board *the Blue Pearl*. He had taken care of many amputations in order to prevent gangrene from sitting in on many a man. He had replaced Captain Stanvic's eye with a glass eye that had been gouged out in a fight several years ago. It did not serve any purpose but it did serve as an advantage as far not having to wear a patch on his eye. Dr. Agnes knew that was part of his job.

Christen was taken to the medic quarters where Dr. Agnes poured alcohol into the wound to disinfect it. He gave Christen several shots of rum for an anesthetic so he could dig the bullet out of his leg. After finishing, he wrapped the wound in a bandana and tied it tightly so that it would not fall off. Dr. Agnes had been in the profession long enough to know that it did not take long for infection to sit in on a tightly populated ship at sea.

By now, Leevin was feeling sick. He was acting demented and running around the ship like a chicken with his head twisted off. It wasn't until he had been tied down on the doctors table that it was discovered that he had drank some sea water that had been put in barrels for the ships mates to bathe in. These barrels had been mistakenly placed in the galley marked as broth barrels, in which Leevin had helped himself to plenty of it.

This absolutely angered Captain Stanvic. "How could some one have caused such a mistake to happen?" He asked himself." "Whoever is found guilty for doing this," Captain Stanvic muttered under his breath, "will pay dearly."

Chapter 11

Dr. Agnes Operates

The chaos on the ship was certainly getting out of control. People were scurrying about in dismay at what was happening to Christen and Leevin. Christen had passed out from all the rum. Leevin had already escaped the ropes that had been holding him down on Dr. Agnes' bed. Fredrick and Donovan had carried him down to the brig for his own safety.

Donovan was usually perched high atop the crows nest. He had a very keen eye for enemy ship coming into the same waters. He never packed much to bring on the ship because the telescope he used was gigantic in size. It was quiet a task climbing the ropes with it and getting it to the top of the crows nest.

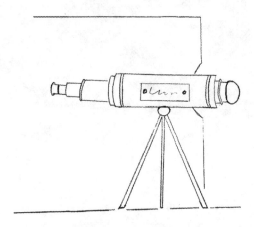

This was Donovan's fifth voyage. His wife back home was showing belly so he was looking forward to getting the voyage done and getting back home to her. This would be their first child.

At daybreak, the next day the mood on board *the Blue Pearl* was still grim. Leevin was not doing well at all. Dr. Agnes had been up all night soaking wet towels to keep his fever down and to allow him to get water from sucking on them. Leevin was much too feverish and dehydrated to lift head from his pillow.

Infection had begun to sit in on Christens wound. Red streaks were running down his leg and liquid was beginning to seep from it. Dr. Agnes would have to amputate his leg by morning or Christen would be in danger of gangrene setting in.

Captain Stanvic's mood was low. He had been up all night navigating the ship since Leevin's illness. He had shut his captain's door earlier not wanting to be bothered by anyone. He had come out for an early morning meal of fruit and ham. After eating, he returned to the captain's seat to sit alone and to ponder what kind of punishment should be given to someone making such a tragic fatal mistake causing such sickness upon one of his men.

Delphin, come up on deck and knocked on Captain Stanvic's door. When Captain Stanvic opened the door, Delphin handed him a book. After looking inside the book, he realized that it was a journal belonging to Privateer Lance Pace. Inside the journal, the last entry made was one of pure mutiny.

Privateer Pace had written in his last entry that he had brought the barrel up and placed it out for Leevin to drink. He knew that His Majesty knew nothing of Leevin being co-captain of the ship. Therefore, if he eliminated Leevin it would only leave Captain Stanvic to navigate the trip. He could then mutineer the ship when Captain Stanvic became too tired to continue. He would not lose any pay if His Majesty did not know that Leevin was Captain Stanvic's co-captain or that he had eliminated him.

Privateer Pace's plan had worked but it was a little late on the draw for him. Not once had Captain Stanvic feared any of his crew he would take out until this voyage. He could no longer continue to be their friend-he had to be their captain.

The ship was coming up to the port of the Merchants reload. They could see already that they were not welcomed. Captain Stanvic had no expectations of being welcomed there anyway. He let down board and he and all his men stood gazing callously at the merchants who appeared to be armed and waiting.

Captain Stanvic always tried to be a fair man, so he gave the merchants one chance to listen to his offer or face being stormed by bullets and slashed by swords. Unusually, they agreed to listen. He had offered them twenty gold bars to supply his boat and to provide bandanas and bandages for the wounds that Christen had sustained.

Unlike what Captain Stanvic had expected, the merchants agreed and the ship was loaded. Captain Stanvic and his men carried on to sea with a little less dreariness.

Chapter 12

The Pirates Code of Conduct

Leevin could no longer hold on. He had fallen short to his sickness. Christen would be facing amputation of his leg. Before being sent to the surgery room, all of his shipmates gathered in his room. He was given a jug of rum to drink and his shipmates had been given a shot of rum to wish him their best and to send him on his way.

At high noon, Dr. Agnes began taking Christens leg off. He was grateful that he did not have to amputate above his knee. Captain Stanvic stayed close by to comfort his compadre. The task took long grueling hours. The pain was unbearable. After stitching him back up, Dr. Agnes sit down to have a drink for his self. This work paid well but it did leave a nightmare or two inside your head.

The next day it was off to a completely different atmosphere. It would be one of mystery and darkness. It was definitely not a safe place to land a ship and let your guard down.

Lynica was a foul country. It was home to all the pirates, buccaneers, mutineers, and privateers. It was home to those who had been marooned by their shipmates due to some sort of defiance of their ships Pirates Code of Conduct. This Code of Conduct states the rules of the individual ship. If broken, one would possibly face death. They could also face being abandoned on a deserted island or cast out into enemy territory.

All of the seamen had to sign this code of conduct before being allowed to board the ship. If they refused to sign this, then Captain would simply not allow them to embark on this expedition. Captain Stanvic's Code of Conduct was not quiet as harsh as most captain's orders were. Captain Stanvic had yet to punish anyone for breaking these rules.

the Blue Pearl
Capt. Michael Stanvic

Pirate Code of Conduct

· Everyone shall obey orders.

· Booty will be shared as follows:
  -1 share to every seaman;
  -1½ shares to the captain;
  -1¼ shares to the second captain and gunner.

· The punishment for hitting a man is 20 lashes to the bare back.

· Anyone being lazy will lose his share of booty.

· All seamen may vote on important decisions.

· Everyone may have a share of fresh food + water.

· The punishment for stealing is death.

· The compensation for losing a limb is 500 silver dollars; an eye 200.

X _____

Chapter 13

Leevin is laid to Rest

Their first stop, as bad as they loathed the ideal, was at the pirate graveyard to plant their friend Leevin. They all gathered around the empty grave. Each of them said a solemn prayer for their shipmate's soul. They took turns misting his grave with rum as they lowered his body. He has now been released to Davy Jones' locker.

Empty barrels, which were being used as tables were sitting next to the burial site. Several of the crewmembers were playing cards while soft music was playing by the musician on board. The spirits were being passed around to celebrate the life of a friend they had shared and lost. Leevin was a good man and everyone who had the chance to be friends with him will miss him dearly.

May he rest in peace?

Captain Stanvic and Feathers had wandered off from his fellow shipmates. This had been the site for the ending of many a man of his kind. It was about the only friendly part of this ghastly country of Lynica.

Lynica was home to Plank Lake and the appalling town of Skullville. Plank Lake was notorious for many a Captains fooling many of their shipmates into diving into the dark waters for treasures that did not exist. The captains would then sail off into the horizon leaving them behind along with their dreams of finding a great treasure to return back home to their families with.

In the summertime, when the sun was closest to earth, the smell of death was vicious. The river would drop during drought season and the skulls and skeletons of the tricked pirates would be lying just feet from the river's edge.

Women and children did not live in Lynica in fear of losing their lives. There was also the fear of their young boys growing up to be pirates. The biggest fear though was that if they did live there that they would end up having to pay for the wrongdoings of their husbands, fathers, and their sons.

Farming was completely impossible because the land was a creation of molten lava. Sand was scarce but not as scarce as soil. Trees were a minority due to the scarcity of the soil. Vegetation did not grow at all. Caves were abundant which did allow for cool shelter for the few men who lived in the country.

Sunrise colony was just that. It was very hot and very humid. Had it not been adjoining the Raven Ocean it would not have been habitable at all. It was home to the biggest majority of people who scarcely populated this country.

Raven Ocean had provided the people of Sunrise Colony a major supply of fish, crabmeat, and lobster. Seaweed was a favorite of the townsfolk because it was about the only greens in their diets. Sharks were used for oil and for their meat. It was not very often they could capture them because it was just too risky. Sea turtles were protected so the people of Sunrise Colony never harmed them. If anyone were caught harming a sea turtle they would face death by hanging.

Chapter 14

The Poisoned Frogs

The burial service for their lost crewmate had ended and the men began to hike back to the ship. Snakes of many colors were crawling across the lava rocks. Some of them were scurrying away quickly. Some of them were stopping to hiss or to shake a rattle at the men.

John was leading the men back when unexpectedly he fell over as if he had just died. The men froze in suspense as to what had just happened to him. They all quickly pulled together and ran to his rescue.

A poisonous frog had bitten John. It was lying underneath him when the other men rolled him over. They all jumped back in fear that they were to be the next victim. Nobody would have dreamed that this was going to happen. Sherlin grabbed from her side a pistol she always carried with her for protection and began to fire at the poisonous creature. With one shot, she had taken the life right out of it.

To the left of her she saw another and to her right she saw another one. She cocked her pistol and fired twice taking them both out within barely two seconds. The men had come to realize that Sherlin was serious about wanting to become one of them.

They all began working to save John. They tied a bandana as a tourniquet around his leg to stop the poison from spreading throughout entire system. He had already begun to complain that he could not feel any part of his body.

Dr. Agnes who had been at the back of the company of pirates had now made his way to him. He did not have any training in what to do if such a thing as this had happened. He did however jump hurriedly into thinking that he could maybe treat it the same as a poisonous snakebite.

For their safety they were going to have to think rapidly before anymore of them had to be exposed to another attack from the frogs or even a snake attack. They were all hoping that Dr. Agnes could save John's life.

The men on the ship had grown to like John a great deal. He had been the one who seemed to hold the crowd together at suppertime each evening. John was the one who kept everyone's spirits high on hopes of finding a very valuable treasure.

Losing John would be a very big blow to the pirate's spirits. They had already lost Leevin and Christen had not been able to attend the burial services. He had not completely healed from the amputation he had to have from the bullet wound he sustained at Leepers Plantation. He had stayed back on board *the Blue Pearl* awaiting his shipmates return.

Dr. Agnes pulled from his journey pack that he always carried with him, a small, sharp, single edge knife and began to cut away the flesh on John's leg. He cut deeply to ensure that he had removed enough of the flesh so that no poison would remain in his system.

John was squealing in anguish and no amount of rum or any kind of spirits could comfort that kind of hurt. He would have to just get a grip and bear the pain if he wanted to survive such a deadly attack. He knew Dr. Agnes was a good doctor and that he would do all he could to save his life and to save his leg.

After just a few moments, Dr. Agnes was finishing cutting away Johns wound. He finished by pouring some alcohol into the large hole and covering it with a large piece of gauze. He would not know if he had saved John's life until he removed the bandana that he was using to seal off the poison to the rest of his body.

Slowly he removed the bandana from his leg. To everyone's amazement, John was pulling right out of this fateful ordeal. The feeling to the rest of John's limbs was slowly returning.

Chapter 15

The Blue Pearl is Stolen

Everyone helped in any way; they could to get John back to shore where they had left the ship. Thomas went ahead of the group to ensure the pirates that it was safe to continue.

Dawson was one of the bravest men Captain Stanvic had ever met. He had been in many battles and had yet to lose a limb. Thomas did have his fair share of scars.

Dawson had come to a sudden halt when he noticed probably the most horrifying thing anyone could have ever imagined. Their ship, *the Blue Pearl*, was now being stolen. In the near horizon, it was easy to see it drifting back into the high seas.

The men were outraged now. How were they supposed to get to the treasure or even get back home without the ship? Captain Stanvic and Red Head Fred began to come up with a quick plan.

Thomas was exiled from the Queen Island Army after he was accused of stealing jewels from the Queen. To this day, he denies it but he was found with them and that made him guilty to everyone else's eye. His story was that he had rescued them from the vagrant who had stolen them and was planning to return them to Her Majesty.

They quickly began collecting driftwood and tying them together with ropes. They could only make three rafts because that was all the rope they had with them.

The strongest and quickest men were to board the rafts and float out to *the Blue Pearl.* The rest would stay behind and hope that the ship would be rescued, so that they could get back on board and continue the journey to the buried treasure.

The men were quick to sneak up on the large vessel and within no time, they were beginning to board it. As they sneaked over to the Cannons they over took the first man at arms. He was not a small man and it took three men to take him down quietly.

They quickly tied and blind folded him. They also gagged him in order to keep him from ratting on them. Next, they headed amidship to see who would be next for them to take out. They were about to have the biggest surprise of all standing before them.

Sir Lance Pace and several of his armed soldiers were holding carriage waiting for their strike. This confrontation had been unexpected.

Sir Lance looked most modest when he nodded his head to his men to begin attack. He waved a solid red flag declaring war. His innocence had never been much because he was always guilty of causing confrontation wherever he was. Even if there was not a problem, he was sure to make one.

Captain Stanvic yelled to his men "forward mates, lets get the ship back now!" "I am authorizing any acts of violence you have in your soul to be let out now," he added. "May the saints be with each of us!" he screamed.

The men began to pull their cat of nine tails out, their swords, cans of exploding gunpowder and their guns. The fight was on and Sir Lance

Pace would have to die for all the turmoil he had caused to their ship. To get to him they had to overcome his soldiers in which they had set their minds to fight them with all they had in them.

The swords were clanging loud enough to hurt anyone's ears. Fredrick made the first hit he had taken out the first soldier to step up to battle. He and Captain Stanvic began to charge into the fierce looking soldiers. They had their guns cocked and began to firing fiercely. Captain Stanvic, most of the time he was at sea, would have eighteen pistols hanging from his neck. All of them would be loaded and ready to fire.

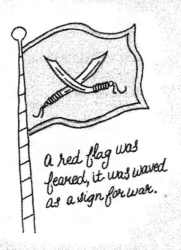

a red flag was feared, it was waved as a sign for war.

Captain Stanvic had taken out twelve men in less than two minutes into battle. He was lightly cut on his upper right arm but that would stop him now. He continued to fight his way through the soldiers trying to make passage to Sir Lance Pace.

Sherlin, unknowingly to Captain Stanvic, had made her way on board to help her shipmates fight. Captain Stanvic was furious to see her there. Sherlin had been like a daughter to him and he did not want to see her hurt. It frustrated him that he could not express his anger to her right now and that he would have to hope that she would not injured.

Sherlin struck the first in command soldier across the neck with a bayonet that she had taken from John's shroud. He collapsed as soon as she had done this. The soldiers of Sir Lance Pace had seen. It angered them and they all turned and began to take aim at her.

Alex, who had been very fond of Sherlin but was too introverted to let her know, he began firing over and around her to keep the soldiers back. He began yelling for Fredrick to come to his aid. Fredrick would have to light and throw some cans of exploding gunpowder into the midst of the aggressive soldiers.

After Fredrick threw in the cans of exploding gunpowder, Sherlin ran over to where he and Alex were standing. Alex was screaming for her to make way to the galley and stay put until the battle was over. Sherlin did not like the ideal but she did as she had been ordered.

Captain Stanvic had made way to Sir Lance Pace. Fighting him would not be easy. He was a ten star general in sword fighting back in King Island. Captain Stanvic would have to keep that in mind as he began to fight him.

Captain Stanvic would have to defeat him. There would be no room for losing now. What Sir Lance Pace did not know was that Captain Stanvic still had six live shots left in his pistols, and Sir Lance had already spent all his bullets.

They were swinging left to right, each one ducking to miss the other ones sword. They were neck and neck and each one was as good as the other. Captain Stanvic's men were in fear of losing their great leader.

Sir Lance Pace had lost his entire backup and it was down to him or Captain Stanvic and his crew winning this battle. Sir Lance knew that killing Captain Stanvic would mean sudden death for him and there was no way of escaping the ship to stay alive. Therefore, his decision to continue and fight to his death was just that.

Captain Stanvic swung his sword fiercely at Sir Lance Pace so hard he sliced through his left leg. Sir Lance retaliated with a blow back so hard it nearly cut Captain Stanvic's hand off and caused him to lose balance and fall to the floor.

Looking up Captain Stanvic saw death looking at him in the eye. He reached and grabbed his pistol that had fallen off during the duel and pulled the trigger. Sir Lance Pace fell to his knees and then onto his face. He is now located in Davy Jones' locker.

Chapter 16

Dominic Becomes Second Captain

The ship had been rescued and that was the best feeling of all. No matter what they had to overcome, they had won this battle and they would not be deserted in such an uninhabitable country.

Dr. Agnes rushed to Captain Stanvic and immediately began tying off Captain Stanvic's wound. He would certainly lose his hand but that was better than losing his life or any of his crew's life.

Dominic had gone to captain Stanvic's night quarters to check on Feathers. With all greatness, Feather's had not been harmed at all. He opened his cage and put out his hand for Feathers to perch on. Dominic then took him to the doctor's quarters for Captain Stanvic to see and to brighten his dreadful day a little.

Dominic had been an angler back in Stanson for several years. Fishing had been such a great industry for a while but the fish had started becoming scarce due to the commercialism of the fish markets. He had some experience in navigation and Captain Stanvic had asked him to navigate the ship until he could get his strength back after the amputation of his hand.

Dominic turned the ship around and returned to shore to pick up the crew that had been left there. They were all ecstatic to see the return of their ship.

Chapter 17

Sherlin Admits Her Fears

Cleanup on board was steadily taking place. The bodies of Sir Lance Pace and his men were had been thrown overboard. Normally it would be Delphin's job to clean deck, but the mess left from the battle was massive. Everyone had to join in cleaning this gruesome mess up.

Alex had gone to the galley to make sure Sherlin was doing well. Sherlin was not doing well at all. She Confided in Alex that she had been afraid out on the deck earlier. Sherlin had put herself into that danger and she regretted having done so. All her life she had wanted to be a pirate and today she decided that her place on the pirate ship was in the galley.

Alex explained to her that what she does in the galley is just as important as the men who are on deck operating the sails and navigating the ship. He hugged her tightly and wiped the tears from her blood stained face. He promised to her that as long as he was alive that he would see to it that no one would ever harm her.

He and Sherlin washed up and began to prepare supper for all their fellow shipmates. They were going to fix the best-breaded and fried tilapia fish planks anyone had ever eaten. Along with that, they were peeling oranges and bananas and mixing them with grapes to make a fruity cocktail mixed with the best of spirits. The rolls that had come out of the ovens were obese, fluffy, light, and buttery.

Everyone came into the galley looking defeated. John was not eating with them tonight and neither was Captain Stanvic. There was no one to tell exciting stories of piracy, yet each one of them had their own story written deep into their souls now. Stories that were unlike the ones that John had told. His that did not include the realism of guts and glory nor did any of them include stories of losing their shipmates or of shipmates losing their limbs.

Captain Stanvic and Feathers were resting in his cabin. He did not really have much to say to anyone but that everyone should continue with the treasure hunt as planned. They all agreed to continue but to hold anchor for the night.

Linden, who was the musician, changed the mood of the pirates. This night he put the organ up and played the fiddle. He played upbeat, inspirational music. The crowd was clapping and dancing and the spirits they were ingesting only made the harmony ignite into pure enjoyment.

Sherlin was left to clean up after the men had all retired to their hammocks for the night. She was still not ready to retire for the night after having a day like today.

Chapter 18

A Change in Plans

Dominic had awakened early that morning. He pulled the anchors up and began to navigate the ship towards the south. He had decided that it was best to steer away from Skullville due to the malevolent nature of the town.

He navigated the ship to approximately fifty nautical miles from the shore of Skullville. The waters were variable but Dominic could handle it with Fredrick operating the sails. This plan would make it a half a day longer but it would keep the crew safe.

The sun was almost unbearable. It was beaming down upon everyone. The humidity was intense. This was definitely the hottest day they had encountered.

Skullville was now perpendicular to their location and Dominic began to prepare the boat to come back inland. He was going to have to be cautious because there had been tales of ships going missing in these territories. That was how Lostman Land had been given its name.

Lostman Land supposedly was where the buccaneers, lay low waiting for merchant ships to sail through. The buccaneers would play some sort of fraud to gain entry and steal the loot or the cargo from the merchant's ships.

Normally, they did not bother the pirates. That was not always the rule though, and Dominic knew to be leery near these lands. Knowing the territory made it a great deal easier to journey into dangerous territory.

The bad thing was that either they would have to continue the journey through the night or they would have to set anchor. The bad side to setting anchor would be that they would be subjecting themselves to being raided by buccaneers during the night.

Everyone agreed to continue to travel past Lostman Land. They would continue down towards their final stopping point. The thought of being so close to this treasure after sixteen tough days on board this ship was overwhelming to everyone on board.

Chapter 19

Reaching the Treasure

On the eve of the next day, Captain Stanvic had gotten out of bed and joined everyone on this expedition. He was clearly in high spirits to be out of bed and back on his feet. Captain Stanvic had shown to all on board tremendous bravery and excellent leadership qualities.

Ahead approximately five nautical miles was the location of everyone's dream on board. It was as if the sky had lit up with the most beautiful and they were at the end of the and within a small reach of the treasure

The couple of hours it took for them to reach land were probably the longest wait they had ever encountered.

The land was black with jagged lava rocks protruding from the earth's surface everywhere. They did not care though. They were ready to climb any mountain to get to that treasure.

Captain Stanvic called for everyone to halt. They had all taken off in various directions but Captain Stanvic was holding in his hand the map his grandfather had left him. At the bottom of the map it read:

Fifty paces east, 10 paces north, and 5 paces east.

He informed them that not only might they listen to his orders on how to find this treasure but that they should grab a shovel and follow him to it. They did as he said and began to follow him.

Just as his grandfather had left on the map, the treasure chest was exactly as marked. The shipmates all looked at each other and the excitement was unbelievable. Inside this chest was gold bars and gold dust. There were pearls in the form of necklaces and in the form of earrings. There were gold and silver coins of and unimaginable quantity. There were jewels of all types. There were rubies, emeralds, sapphires and diamonds. These were the most exquisite gems any man could have laid his eyes on.

The chest was loaded onto the ship and all the crewmates headed back to where they had begun this journey at the Port of St. Kasen. To avoid putting themselves in danger going back, they would sail at the least one hundred nautical miles from shore.

Upon returning to port, Captain Stanvic thanked his crew for a job well done and handed to each one as they left the ship, their share of the treasure.

As Captain Stanvic put *the Blue Pearl* to rest at dock, he smiled to his self and gently patted Feathers across his back. This had been the treasure of a lifetime and his grandfather would definitely be most proud of him. He could now take care of his family and his crew could live the lives they had been thirsting for.

Pirate Vocabulary

Abaft.....................to the rear of the ship
Abeam......at right angles of the ship
About.......around, as in "come about"
Aft......................at the back of the ship
Ahoy...hello!
Aloft......up in the rigging
Amidships......in the center of the ship
Avast......stop
Aye, aye......yes
Bail......to remove water by bucket
Bow........................the front of a ship
Brig......holding cell for prisoners
Cabin boy.................young man chosen to keep the deck clean and dry
Cast off....................let go
Davy Jones' locker....graveyard or resting place after death
Fore......at the front of the ship
Galley......kitchen
Gangways......get out of the way
Jolly Roger......the infamous Pirate's flag
Larboard....................the left side of the ship looking forward
Look lively.......get busy
Me hearties.......my crewmates
Quarters......living area
Rudder......used to steer the ship
Sea anchor......a drag behind the ship for slowing it
Sea chest......a box containing a sea staffs belongings
Shake a leg..................get them feet moving, also dancing
Show a leg...................get up and get busy
Stern......the rear of the ship
Swab the deck.......mop the deck